F+P-J

We Work at the
Fire Station

Angela Aylmore

Heinemann Library
Chicago, Illinois

Customer Service   888-454-2279
Visit our website at www.heinemannlibrary.com

Photo research by Erica Newbery
Designed by Jo Hinton-Malivoire and bigtop
Printed in China by South China Printing Company

10 09 08 07
10 9 8 7 6 5 4 3

Library of Congress Cataloging-in-Publication Data
Aylmore, Angela.
  We work at the fire station / Angela Aylmore.
     p. cm. -- (Where we work)
  Includes bibliographical references and index.
  ISBN 1-4109-2243-X (library binding - hardcover) -- ISBN 1-4109-2248-0 (pbk.)
  ISBN 978-1-4109-2243-4 (library binding - hardcover) -- ISBN 978-1-4109-2248-9 (pbk.)
  1. Fire extinction--Juvenile literature. 2. Fire stations--Juvenile literature. 3. Fire fighters--Juvenile literature.
I. Title. II. Series.
TH9148.A885 2006
628.9'2--dc22

                                2005033275
Acknowledgments
The author and publisher are grateful to the following for permission to reproduce copyright material:
Alamy pp. **6–7** (Ace Stock Limited), **20** (Blue Shadows); Corbis pp. **4–5** (George Hall), **8** (Robert Maass) **11**, **12**, **13** (Joseph Sohm/ ChromoSohm Inc.), **14–15** (Ted Horowitz); Getty Images pp. **17** (Photodisc), **20** top (Photodisc); Photoedit p. **21** top (Bill Aron); Shout pp. **18–19**. Quiz pp. **22–23**: **astronaut** (Getty/Photodisc), **brush and comb** (Corbis/DK Limited), **doctor** (Getty Images/Photodisc), **firefighter helmet** (Corbis), **ladder** (Corbis/Royalty Free), **scrubs** (Corbis), **space food** (Alamy/Hugh Threlfall), **stethoscope** (Getty Images/Photodisc), **thermometer** (Getty Images/Photodisc).

Cover photograph of a firefighter reproduced with permission of Corbis/Ted Horowitz.

Some words are shown in bold, **like this**. They are explained in the glossary on page 24.

Contents

Welcome to the Fire Station!

This is a fire station.

Who do you think
works here?

Working in a Fire Station

We are fire fighters. We work at the fire station.

6

The Alarm

The **alarm** rings when there is a fire.

RING!!!

ZOOOOM!

The pole helps us to get downstairs quickly.

Getting Dressed

We have to wear special clothes.

They keep us safe from smoke and flames.

helmet

mask

jacket

gloves

boots

All Aboard the Fire Engine!

This is a fire engine.

ladders

hose reel

Using a Fire Hose

We use water to
put out most fires.

We spray the water from a fire **hose**.

15

Using Ladders

Some buildings are very tall.

We use ladders
to help us
rescue people.

Back at the Station

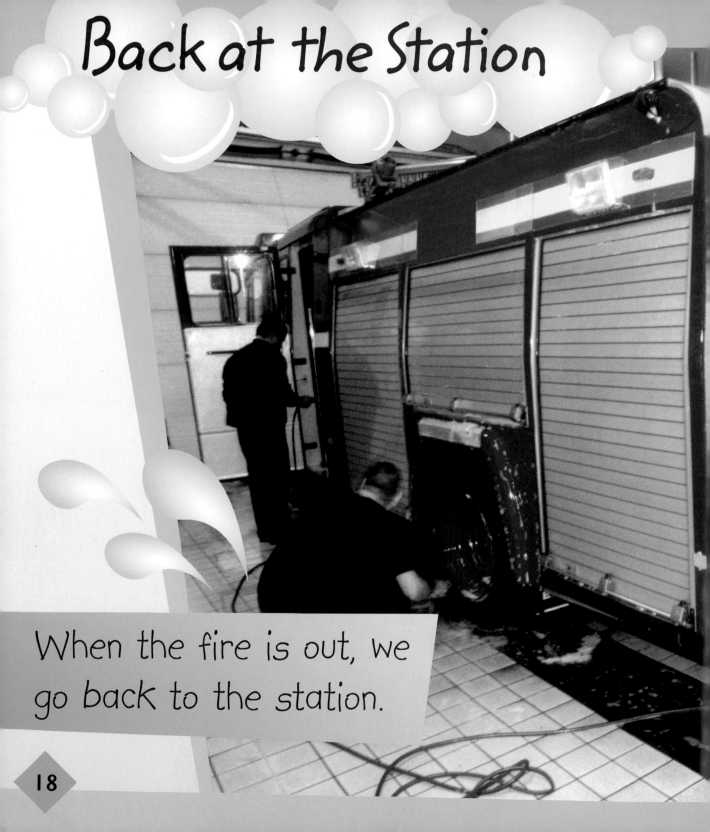

When the fire is out, we go back to the station.

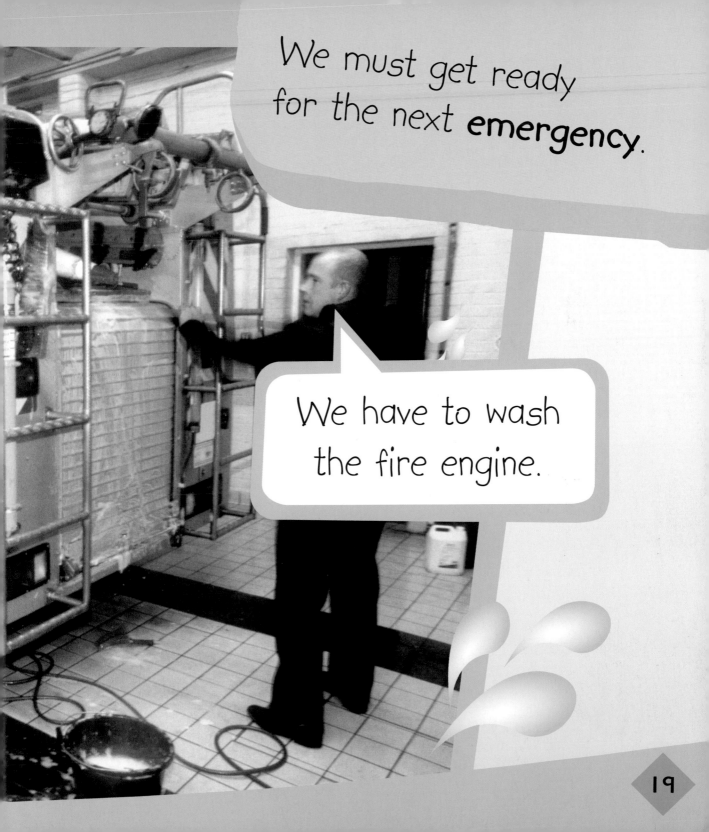

We must get ready for the next **emergency**.

We have to wash the fire engine.

Staying Safe

Never play with **matches** or anything hot.
You might start a fire.

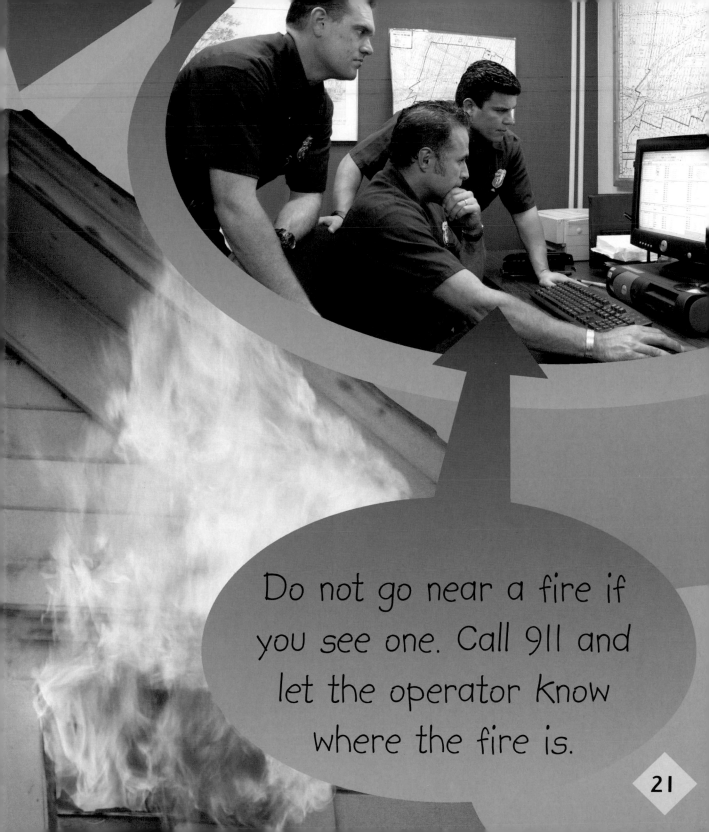

Do not go near a fire if you see one. Call 911 and let the operator know where the fire is.

Quiz

space food

Do you want to be a fire fighter? Which of these things would you need?

stethoscope

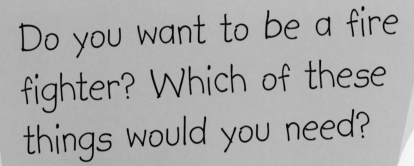
spacesuit

helmet

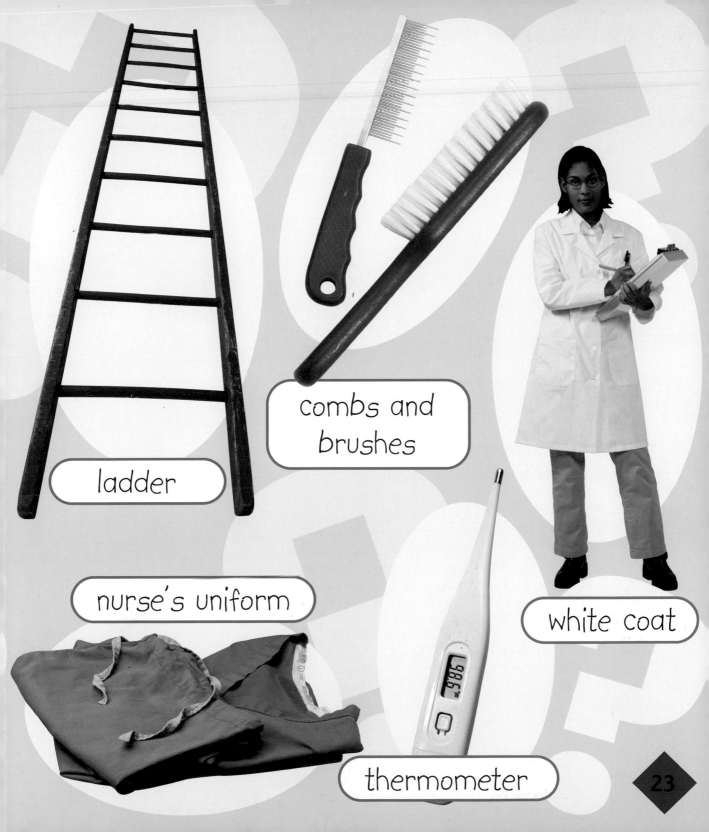

ladder

combs and brushes

nurse's uniform

white coat

thermometer

23

Glossary

alarm loud bell that rings

emergency something serious and sudden

hose long, bendable pipe that carries water

matches short stick of wood for making a fire

rescue save

siren loud noise that a fire engine makes

Index

Notes for Adults

This series supports the young child's exploration of their learning environment and their knowledge and understanding of their world.

The series shows the different jobs that professionals do in four different environments. There are opportunities to compare and contrast the jobs and provide an understanding of what each entails.

The books will help the child to extend their vocabulary, as they will hear new words. Some of the words that may be new to them in **We Work at the Fire Station** are *emergency*, *alarm*, *siren*, *hose*, *flames*, *rescue*, and *smoke*. Since the words are used in context in the book, this should enable the young child to gradually incorporate them into their own vocabulary.

Follow-up Activities
The child could role play situations at a fire station. They could imagine the different emergencies a fire fighter might encounter, such as putting out a fire or rescuing an animal. The child could also record what they have found out by drawing, painting, or tape recording their experiences.

24